D0577683

Dear Parent:
Your child's love of reading starts here!

Every child learns to read in a different way and at his or her own speed. Some go back and forth between reading levels and read favorite books again and again. Others read through each level in order. You can help your young reader improve and become more confident by encouraging his or her own interests and abilities. From books your child reads with you to the first books he or she reads alone, there are I Can Read Books for every stage of reading:

SHARED READING
Basic language, word repetition, and whimsical illustrations, ideal for sharing with your emergent reader

BEGINNING READING
Short sentences, familiar words, and simple concepts for children eager to read on their own

READING WITH HELP
Engaging stories, longer sentences, and language play for developing readers

READING ALONE
Complex plots, challenging vocabulary, and high-interest topics for the independent reader

I Can Read Books have introduced children to the joy of reading since 1957. Featuring award-winning authors and illustrators and a fabulous cast of beloved characters, I Can Read Books set the standard for beginning readers.

A lifetime of discovery begins with the magical words "I Can Read!"

Visit www.icanread.com for information
on enriching your child's reading experience.

The Berenstain Bears and the Ghost of the Theater
Copyright © 2020 by Berenstain Publishing, Inc.

Library of Congress Control Number: 2019936835
ISBN 978-0-06-265475-5 (trade bdg.) — ISBN 978-0-06-265474-8 (pbk.)

Book design by Chrisila Maida
20 21 22 23 24   SCP   10 9 8 7 6 5 4 3 2 1   ❖   First Edition

The Berenstain Bears®
and the GHOST OF THE THEATER

Mike Berenstain

Based on the characters created by
Stan and Jan Berenstain

HARPER
An Imprint of HarperCollinsPublishers

Brother and Sister Bear are looking
for a summer job.
They see a sign outside the theater,
"Helpers wanted."
They go inside.

Mr. Bruno runs the theater.

"We saw your sign," says Brother.

"Good," says Mr. Bruno.

"You can help clean up.

Grab a broom."

Brother and Sister sweep

the big, empty theater.

Honey helps them.

They sweep the backstage.

It is dark and spooky.

There are many props backstage.

Props are things used in a play.

There are fake swords and spears.

There's a suit of armor.

There are paintings and statues.

The cubs find a stuffed bird.

It is sitting on a statue's head.

"Creepy!" says Sister.

The cubs find a big black pot.

It is a prop for a play

about witches.

Brother stirs the pot with his broom.

"Double, double,

toil and trouble!" he says.

"Stop that!" says Sister.

"It's scary!"

"Toil and trouble!" says Brother.

"Stop it!" says Sister.

"Toil and trouble!"

says another voice.

"Who said that?" asks Brother.

"Toil and trouble!" says the voice.

The cubs see two

glowing, yellow eyes!

"YEOW!" yell the cubs.

They run away!

They run into Mr. Bruno.

"We saw a ghost!" says Brother.

"Of course," says Mr. Bruno.

"That's the Ghost of the Theater.

Come, we'll meet him."

"We don't want to meet a ghost!"

says Sister.

"Don't worry," says Mr. Bruno.

"He's a friendly ghost."

They go backstage.

"Where's the ghost?" asks Brother.

"Right here," says Mr. Bruno.

He points to the stuffed bird.

"Toil and trouble!" croaks the bird.

The cubs laugh.

"We thought he was stuffed!"
says Sister.

"Meet Hamlet, our theater pet,"
says Mr. Bruno.

"He will be in our next play.

Would you like to be in it with him?"

"Yes, we would!" says Brother.

Shakesbeare~

Brother, Sister, and Honey

are in the next play.

They are witches' helpers.

30

Hamlet sits on Brother's shoulder.

"Toil and trouble!" he croaks.

The play is a hit.

Everyone claps and cheers.

Brother, Sister, Honey,

and Hamlet take a bow.